Puppy Makes Friends

written by Dr. Mary Manz Simon

illustrated by Kathy Couri

© 2003 Mary Manz Simon. © 2003 Standard Publishing, Cincinnati, Ohio. A division of Standex International Corporation. All rights reserved. Sprout logo is a trademark of Standard Publishing. First Virtues™ is a trademark of Standard Publishing. Printed in Italy. Project editor: Jennifer Holder. Design: Robert Glover and Suzanne Jacobson. Scripture quoted from the *HOLY BIBLE, Contemporary English Version*. Copyright © 1995 by American Bible Society. Used by permission. ISBN 0-7847-1414-2

09 08 07 06 05 04 03   9 8 7 6 5 4 3 2 1

Standard Publishing

cincinnati, ohio

www.standardpub.com

Puppy, Puppy,
share today,
what the Bible
has to say...

Friendly means
to understand
when a person
needs a hand.

When does friendship
really start?
When you share love
from your heart.

Playing ball
is lots more fun
when I'm not
the only one.

If a friend
falls in a race,
I will wipe tears
from his face.

I show I am
friendly, too,
when I talk
with someone new.

My new friend
begins to smile,
after we
have played awhile.

When I'm friendly,
then I share,
for that shows
I really care.

God is always
there for you.
He wants to be
your friend, too.

"A friend is always a friend."
Proverbs 17:17

Friendship Friendship Friendship Friendship

Friendship Friendship Friendship Friendship

Friendship Friendship Friendship Friendship

Friendship Friendship Friendship Friendship

Friendship Friendship Friendship Friendship

Friendship Friendship Friendship Friendship

Friendship Friendship Friendship Friendship